samurai

courage

Time Soldiers®
Book #6 SAMURAI

Text © 2006 Kathleen Duey
Photography © 2006 Robert Gould
Digital Illustrations © 2006 Eugene Epstein

Library of Congress Control Number: 2005935054
ISBN: 1-929945-62-0

Printed in USA

Reading is more fun with
BiG GUY BOOKS Inc.
www.bigguybooks.com

Published by BiG GUY BOOKS, Inc.
Carlsbad, CA, USA

Check out the cool stuff at www.bigguybooks.com

SAMURAI

Book # 6 in the TIME SOLDIERS® Series

By KATHLEEN DUEY

Created & Photographed by
ROBERT GOULD

Digital Illustration & 3D Special Effects by
EUGENE EPSTEIN

One rainy morning, six neighborhood kids find a time portal in the woods. Through swirling green light, they can see a living dinosaur! They can't convince their parents the portal exists, so they pack their camping gear and go through it, armed with a videocamera. They outrun Velociraptors, and outwit a T-Rex—and make it home with an incredible videotape.

Brian has made a tough decision. He's been accepted into special classes that will qualify him for a scholarship. Since he has to study so much, the Time Soldiers are looking for someone to replace him. They are all working to stay fit, research times and places they want to explore, and learn survival skills while they decide where to go next.

PATCH

GREEN STONE

TIME PORTAL ENTRANCE

AMULET

ARTHUR

REX

GREEN BROOCH

MUMMY

But before they can show it to anyone, a mysterious man in a dark suit and sunglasses steals it. The portal opens the very next day. Then nearly a year goes by before it transports them back in time again. Dinosaurs, pirates, knights, a boy pharaoh in ancient Egypt: With every adventure, the Time Soldiers learn more about history, about

The men in dark suits are watching the Time Soldiers very closely. They know why the four oldest kids—Jon, Adam, Rob and Mariah—can't go through the portal anymore. They know about the strange green stones. And they know that time is running out… .

The library was quiet. "I can't decide," Luke was saying. "I want to go a hundred places." He noticed a girl sitting nearby and gestured. "She's here every

"She's good at martial arts, too," Bernardo said. "I've seen her practicing at the dojo."

Luke leaned forward. "We should find out more

4

Outside, Mikey introduced everyone. "My name's Nami," the girl said. "I've noticed you studying together. Is it a class project?"

Bernardo glanced at Mikey, then shook his head. "Not exactly. I've seen you at the dojo."

Nami nodded. "I want to do movie stunts when I grow up—I'll need to know martial arts."

Everyone liked Nami and they talked to her more each day. Finally, they decided to ask her to become a Time Soldier. She looked amazed—and excited.

"Could we go to Edo, the city that became Tokyo?" Nami asked, "I speak Japanese and I have samurai ancestors."

"Samurai?" Mikey asked. Bernardo and Luke smiled

Two men in dark suits and mirrored sunglasses stared at the organic diode screen. The picture was perfect. "Should we get the stone now?" one asked.

The other frowned. "Why? They will find more pieces of it and—"

"Or they could lose it," the first man said.

"They won't," the second man said. "And we need at least—"

"I'm tired of waiting," his friend cut him off. "Is the new girl working out?"

The second man nodded. "And her father owns a film production company. No more costume problems. We should have thought of that."

"We're all getting better," Bernardo said after class. "Our research is nearly done. We're almost ready."

"The Samurai fascinate me," Nami said. "They were always trying to serve, to protect. But I'm a little afraid," she added. "You've done this before, but I can barely believe it's true."

"Everyone is a little scared," Mikey said, then he smiled. "We always stick together and we get home safe. And this time, you'll be able to translate for us."

Nami nodded. "I can't wait."

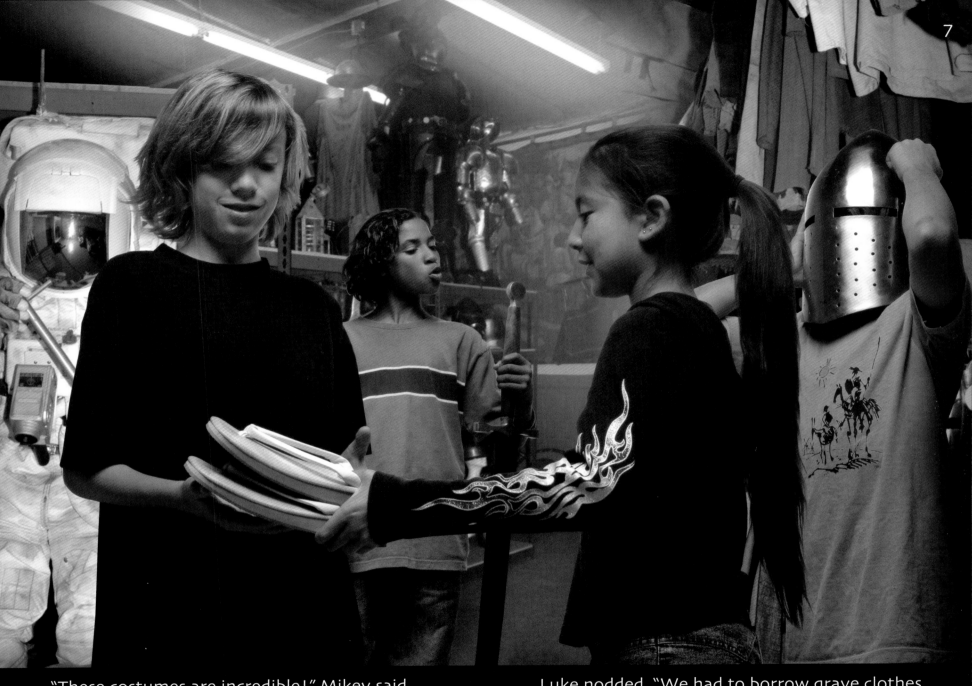

"These costumes are incredible!" Mikey said. "Are you sure your father won't mind?"

Nami smiled. "As long as we take care of everything, no one will even notice. I checked my father's production schedules. They won't need these for a year or more."

Luke nodded. "We had to borrow grave clothes in Egypt. We put them back, but it felt wrong to use them at all. This is going to be so much easier!"

Bernardo laughed. "In medieval England, we actually sewed our camp blankets into robes."

On a sunny Saturday morning, the Time Soldiers changed into their costumes and hiked into the woods. Bernardo held the amulet tightly. He focused his thoughts the way Brian had taught him and closed his eyes for a second.

When he opened them, the portal was waiting. They went in slowly, making sure Nami was all right. She held her breath—it was so strange to be hurtling through time.

When they came out of the swirling green light, they weren't in Edo. They were in a forest above the city. "That's Mount Fuji!" Nami said. "It's so beautiful."

Luke pointed. "I think I see a path that leads in the right direction."
They walked through the forest for hours before they came to a clearing. There was a dojo!

The Time Soldiers walked closer. "Look," Luke whispered, "a samurai teacher and his students!"
Bernardo took a deep breath. "I managed to get us close to the city, but did I miss the time target?"

Mikey shook his head. "No, look at the clothes and the style of swords—we're in the era we studied, around 1700AD."
They all fell silent and watched the samurai working with his class.

The Time Soldiers hid and watched the classes until the sun was low in the sky. Then the samurai teacher started down the path, walking quickly, as though hours of training and teaching had

The Time Soldiers went just fast enough to glimpse the old man now and then. The plum blossoms made the air sweet. "It's so beautiful," Nami said. "I understand why the people here love nature so

An hour passed. Then two. "Did the teacher turn off somewhere?" Bernardo asked.

A moment later, the samurai leapt onto the path, his sword raised. Startled, Bernardo gripped the amulet as Nami began talking to the samurai in

He spoke, then waited as Nami translated.

"I explained that we only followed him to find the city. He says if we camp with him, he'll show us the way in the morning."

"Taro No Yoshiie," the samurai said.

At sunset, the samurai made a campfire and shared his rice and meat. After they had eaten, he asked Nami where they lived. "Far from here," she answered in Japanese. "We came to learn about the samurai."

The old man raised his chin. "Samurai live in peace now. But when I was young, I was in many battles. One was in that clearing." He pointed. Nami translated.

"Would he tell us about it?" Bernardo whispered.

Nami spoke to the old man. He began to talk in a low voice.

The old man's voice was deep and strong. Nami translated.

"When I was young," he said, "I fought to defend my daimyo, my home and my ruler. I served him. I obeyed his orders. It was a hard life, but a proud one. He gave me a helmet for serving well."

"There was a rare stone set in it, the color of fine jade. I wore it the day I was wounded here— and lost it." He stopped, was silent a moment, then went on. "Our enemies fought well. We battled so long that the dust rose like sea mist around us."

Nami listened to what the samurai said, then, when he paused, she repeated it in English. Her eyes were closed. Bernardo watched the samurai's face as he spoke, describing the battle he had been in nearly fifty years before. Luke and Mikey

about losing the helmet. He had been hurt—and he hadn't seen the thief—but someone had stolen the helmet. Another samurai? The old man shook his head. It seemed impossible.

The sunrise woke them all. The samurai led them to a tower, talking to Nami as they walked.

"This is so cool," Luke said as they stood, looking out over the battlefield.

"That's where he lost the helmet," Nami said.

After a moment, the samurai began to speak again. "He's talking about the battle now," Nami said quietly. "And he thanks us for listening to his old tales." She paused. "He says he would be honored to have us in his home."

16

As they followed the old man into Edo, he was talking to Nami. She kept turning back to translate. The samurai explained that the ancient city had begun as a single daimyo. Then other rulers had moved their families and farms closer to the sea. He was proud of his home. In Edo as bright as daylight, and swords that could cut a silk thread dropped upon the blade. Luke turned to Mikey and Bernardo. "We're walking with a real samurai!" They both nodded. It was incredible.

Taro No Yoshiie showed them the shogun's home. It stood like a castle on a hill. The shogun ruled over all the daimyos now, the samurai explained. "Wow," Luke thought to himself, staring at the ancient fortress, thinking about the long history of Edo and all the lives that had begun and ended here.

The old man smiled, then spoke. "He wants to take us through the city now," Nami translated, "before most people are awake." They all knew that the samurai was protecting them and they were grateful.

The samurai led them through shops and businesses. Then he followed one of the canals, walking toward the harbor so they could see the fishing boats. The Time Soldiers kept glancing at each other. It was strange to think that one day this city would be modern Tokyo, full of skyscrapers and cars. When the sun was low in the afternoon sky, the samurai finally led them back to his house.

The old man showed them his gardens. "Some of the bonsai trees are more than 200 years old," Nami said. "His ancestors cared for them."

The samurai's servants prepared food while he talked about the importance of honor. "He's teaching us like we're his students," Mikey whispered. Nami translated and the old man smiled.

After dinner, he showed them his swords and bows, then led them into the tea room. "He wants to honor us with a tea ceremony," Nami said. They all bowed to Taro No Yoshiie. They had read about this—the samurai was giving them an incredible gift.

Once it was dark and the old man had left them, they talked about trying to get his helmet back. They walked outside. Bernardo took the amulet out of his pocket. "I think I can get us to the exact place and time." Nami and Mikey nodded. Bernardo held the amulet tightly and summoned the portal.

In an instant, they were back on the battlefield— and fifty years back in time. The dark of night had vanished. It was a bright morning now and storm clouds were rolling in from the sea.

The two men were staring at their screens.
One of them rubbed his forehead. "We never had adventures like this."
The other man shrugged. "We didn't have time."
There was silence as they both tried not to laugh at the pun. It was true. They had been on assignment and their orders had been very clear.

"I wish we could just leave them alone," the first man said.
The second man didn't bother to answer him. It was impossible and they both knew it. Their orders had not changed.

The sounds of the battle were close, too close. "This way!" Mikey shouted. They ran, then hid near the place the samurai had pointed out—the edge of the meadow where he had lost the helmet. The Time Soldiers were still and silent, watching the men fight. It was like they had fallen into an action movie, but this was real. The warriors were galloping toward their enemies. The archers drew back their bows to take aim... .

"Where is he?" Nami asked over the pounding of the hooves and the shouts of battle.

Then she pointed. "I see him! There he is!"

They all gasped when the samurai slumped forward, then fell from his horse. The helmet rolled downhill. He reached for it, then fell back, closing his eyes. The ringing of swords got louder, mixed with cries of pain and the frantic

"Stay low," Bernardo warned them as the battle surged closer.

"I wish we could tell him that he's going to live, that he'll have a long life," Nami said.

Just as Luke was about to touch the helmet, he glanced up and saw a man running toward him. A ninja? In the blink of an eye, the man grabbed the helmet and rolled to one side. Luke shouted, all his fear turning into anger. This was the man who had stolen the helmet so long ago.

The daimyo had given it to the samurai to honor his courage and loyalty—and this ninja had stolen it!

Luke stood and faced the man. The fire from one of the towers had spread—he could feel the heat of the flames. The ninja stared at him, then turned and ran, fading into the smoke. Luke sprinted back to his friends. They were all talking fast, trying to

"We can't follow a ninja!" Nami was saying. "We'll never manage to keep up. We can't see where he goes and—"

"We can from up there," Luke shouted, pointing at the only tower still standing. An instant later

"Can you see him?" Bernardo asked.

"No," Mikey said. "Wait. There he is, running down the path toward Edo."

Luke frowned. "I really wanted to give that helmet back to the samurai."

"Look," Mikey said. "The ninja's slowing down—he's turning into the forest."

"Spot a landmark," Bernardo said.

Mikey stared. "There's a crooked pine where he turned off. Let's go."

There was a second path, narrow and steep. They followed it downhill. Mikey and Bernardo silently climbed the steps of the little house to make sure the ninja was inside.

"Now what?" Nami whispered when they came back.

"I brought walkie-talkies," Luke said. "And Mikey has stink bombs."

Bernardo reached into the belt pack he wore beneath his kimono. "Two laser pointers, fully charged." Nami was staring at them.

Mikey turned. "We all bring something in case of an emergency. We usually have at least one."

Five minutes later, they had a plan and Mikey had climbed a tree. "Are the lasers bright enough?" he heard Luke ask.

"I think so," Bernardo said. "And it's getting darker."

"Stink bombs work day or night," Mikey joked.

Nami stared up at him. "Aren't you afraid?"

"Sure," he told her as he secured the walkie-talkie.

"We were afraid of the evil knight and the Egyptian temple guards, too." He climbed down. "If everything goes well, we'll be fifty years away from here in a few minutes."

Bernardo glanced at Nami. She looked a little scared, but she seemed steady—she was holding the walkie-talkie firmly in one hand. Good. They

The ninja made a noise inside the little house and Luke jumped, startled. They were all tense. Mikey nodded sharply. "Let's go."

zone 12

unidentified
radio transmitter

(stinkbomb)
updating the
digital
vocabulary

spectrum analyzer

digital rendering in process

zone 07

zone

zone

The men in dark suits were staring at the simulscreens. "I can't believe this," the first man said.
The second man was silent, then he exhaled. "They aren't bringing the stone back are they?"
The first man didn't answer. They both knew the

and stone in it to the old man. They were good-hearted and honest—and they had absolutely no idea what was at stake.

The bright Edo candle lit the whole room. Nami and Bernardo got into position. He lifted his right hand to signal Luke and Mikey. Bernardo took a deep breath and turned the laser pointer on. The light was bright red, and the little cutout on the lens shaped the beam into a dragon. Bernardo angled the light so that the miniature

dragon appeared on the ninja's shoulder, flickered to the wall, then jumped back. The man turned, startled and confused. Bernardo shone the light at the far wall again. "It's working," he whispered to Nami.

Bernardo shifted his position. He shone the dragon-light against the window frame, then aimed it toward the door. The ninja turned to stare at it, then he took a step toward it. Bernardo nodded at Nami, then clicked the laser off. An instant later her voice, low and growling, came through the of the house. Nami sounded cold and stern as she pretended to be the dragon. She was challenging the ninja to a battle. Nami kept her voice low and fierce. "Come out and face us!" she said. "I dare you!"

The ninja stepped outside. Bernardo moved, turning on the second laser. He aimed the lights at the wooden porch beams. Nami knew the ninja had never seen a laser pointer and he had no idea what a walkie-talkie was. To him, the dragon's voice seemed real. "Can you catch us?"

She signaled to Bernardo and he moved the light-dragons from the porch to tree trunks in front of the house.

For a long moment, the ninja followed the light-dragons with his eyes. Then, without warning, he leapt to the ground, his hands raised, ready to fight.

Bernardo lifted the lasers to keep the dragons out of reach as the ninja leapt and spun—then leapt again.

Bernardo kept the light-dragons flickering from tree to tree as the ninja spun and kicked, striking out, trying to defeat them.

Nami glanced up and saw Luke starting toward the window. Good. In a few seconds, he would have the helmet.

40

Luke had to break the window frame to get inside. He grabbed the helmet and climbed back out in seconds. Then he ran for the trees, careful to stay out of the ninja's line of sight. The helmet was heavy and he held it tightly to his chest as

The ninja was still trying to catch the light-dragon. Nami glanced at Bernardo and wrinkled her nose. He nodded. He could smell it, too. Mikey had set off the stinkbombs.

Bernardo moved the light-dragons lower, letting the ninja come closer to them. Then, at the last second, he moved the images to the next tree— and the next—leading the ninja farther from the house, farther from the path. Bernardo glanced back and saw his friends heading uphill. It was time to go. For a few seconds more, Bernardo kept the light-dragons—and the ninja—moving. Then he jammed the laser pointer between two branches and aimed it higher than the ninja could reach—and ran to catch up with the others.

Bernardo held the amulet in his hands and forced himself to concentrate. They had to get back to the samurai, back to the safety of peaceful Edo. Behind them, the ninja spun around at the sound of their footsteps. "Here he comes!" Mikey warned.

Then the portal opened in front of them and they sprinted through it. Coming out into the darkness and silence of the samurai's garden, they all glanced back at the forest on the other side of the swirling green light.

"Can he follow us?" Nami shouted.

"Older kids can't go through without terrible pain," Mikey told her. "We're pretty sure adults can't do it at all."

Bernardo stared at the ninja shoving at the

They all watched as the portal shrank and dimmed, then disappeared, keeping the ninja back in his own time.

"Taro No Yoshiie is going to be so happy to see this," Luke said, holding up the helmet.

"Look at the stone," Mikey said. "It looks like—"

"The stone in the amulet," Bernardo interrupted.

Luke wiped the dust of battle from the stone.

Suddenly, green light snaked between the stones. The helmet dragged Luke forward. He fought to hold on. Mikey helped him and they finally pulled it free, breaking the arc of light. "We need to do some research," Luke said. "Is there a green stone with magnetic properties?"

"One that can also open time portals?" Bernardo added, shaking his head. He put the amulet back in his pocket—the stone felt hot. "Let's go inside," Nami said.

Taro No Yoshiie's eyes went wide when he saw the helmet. "Tell him we wanted to thank him," Mikey said. "We wanted to show our respect and esteem." Nami translated as the samurai took the helmet. His eyes were full of happiness. A few minutes later, he left the room, then came back carrying a beautifully carved box.

"He says it is for us to keep our treasures in," Nami told the others.

The Time Soldiers bowed one last time and said goodbye, then walked a little ways into the woods to open the portal and go home.

"A box?" the first man asked. "Carved and lacquered and—oh no!" As he spoke, the image flickered, then went dark. "They aren't bringing the second stone back, and now they have a box that shields the first one?"

The second man typed quickly, then stood back to read the results. "It's lacquered with cinnabar— imported from China. The lacquer has mercury in it." He turned. "It's like the stone itself is planning all this. Now we'll have to follow them again."

"The dry cleaners mended the little tear in mine," Bernardo told Nami as they hung the kimonos back on the rack. "You can't even see it."

She smiled, then noticed Luke trying on

to a riding school this summer. And we'll need to pick a time and place and—"

"Whoa," Luke

CREDITS

Time Soldiers
Luke - Isiah Jackson
Mikey - Michael Gould
Bernardo - Bernardo Kastlie
Nami - Kiana Pestonjee
Men in Dark Suits - Mark Flanagan, Kelly Shadburn
Young Samurai - Koji Kuninaga
Ninja - Sean Berry
Old Samurai - Master Richard Rabago
Martial Arts Teacher - Bruce Nguyen
Samurai Students - Katherine On
Kenneth Kim, Jae Lee
Cody Mau, Tiffany Le, Calvin Le
Samurai warrior - Master Ken Church

Special Guest Appearance - Briana Vigil

Kathleen Duey - Writer
Robert Gould - Creator/Photographer
Eugene Epstein - Digital Illustrator/Art Director/Story Board Artist
Mahsa Merat, Casting Director
Rakdy Khlok - Research and Costumes
Lara Gurin - Digital Composite Preparation
Jacob Dubizhansky - Digital Composite Preparation
Roman Gurinov - Image Masking
Carol Roland - Editing

Special thanks to:

Aya C. Ibarra - Japan Society of San Diego and Tijuana
Dave Tuites - Japan Society of San Diego Tijuana
Hiroko Johnson - San Diego State Curator, Historical Expert
Joyce Teague - Japanese American Historical Society of San Diego

Costuming and Props
Global Effects, Inc.
Kashu Sales International, Inc.
Aiya, Inc.
E-Bogu.com

TIME SOLDIERS

Robert Gould's **TIME SOLDIERS**
Book #1 **REX**

Robert Gould's **TIME SOLDIERS**
Book #2 **REX²**

Robert Gould's **TIME SOLDIERS**
Book #3 **PATCH**

ROBERT GOULD'S **TIME**